D1450817

THE VALUES LIBRARY

SELF-CONTROL

Having good friends who are positive influences can often make it easier to maintain your self-control.

SELF-CONTROL

Margaret Kneip

THE ROSEN PUBLISHING GROUP, INC.

NEW YORK

Published in 1991 by The Rosen Publishing Group, Inc.
29 East 21st Street, New York, NY 10010.

First Edition
Copyright © 1991 by the Rosen Publishing Group, Inc.

Manufactured in Canada

Library of Congress Cataloging-in-Publication Data

Kneip, Margaret.
    Self-control / Margaret Kneip—1st ed.
    (The Values Library)
    ISBN 0-8239-1228-0
    1. Self-control—Juvenile literature. I. Title. II. Series.
    BF632.K54   1991
    153.8—dc20
                                                                90-23937
                                                                CIP

C O N T E N T S

Saying "no" to your friends takes strength and determination.

JUST SAYING NO

NANCY REAGAN LOOKED UP FROM HER POLISHED MAHOGANY DESK.
She calmly repeated the main point of her sixty-second public-service message: "Listen to me, kids. Don't use drugs. Just say no."

Suzanne Watson watched Mrs. Reagan skeptically. She saw the grand setting of the White House and a woman who had it all. Suzanne thought, "Now, how would she know about drugs?"

The night before, Suzanne had been at a party and had smoked marijuana. Smoking with her friends was something she did often. It was no big thing, except that Suzanne found it hard to concentrate in school the next day. And doing well in school was important to her. She wanted to go to college and study veterinary medicine. She loved taking care of her two dogs. Curing and helping sick animals was her goal in life.

Her guidance counselor, Ms. Crozier, had talked to Suzanne about her failing grades and poor attendance. "Suzanne," she said, "you've got great potential. You're capable of so much more. But some teachers have noticed that when you do make it to class you seem to be dozing off—not there."

"You've got to get it together," Ms. Crozier said. "You're running around too much and with the wrong crowd. Use some self-control."

"Self-control," thought Suzanne. "What is that, and where do I get some? Does it mean 'Just say no'?"

Not exactly. Self-control is being able to control your behavior. It is deciding for yourself how you should act. It is better than simply saying "no" because Nancy Reagan or your teachers or your parents tell you to. They all mean well, of course. But wouldn't you rather control your own behavior than let somebody else tell you what to do?

There are three important reasons for you to have control over your behavior:

- To avoid doing something you will regret later
- To avoid hurting yourself physically or emotionally
- To avoid harming others

In Suzanne's case, she knew that smoking marijuana regularly was causing her to do poorly in school. She often wished that she hadn't smoked the night before when she had a hard time waking up in the morning. She also wondered if the fuzzy feeling in her brain would be permanent—it was there so much now. And she was feeling detached from her family and her responsibilities. Several times she had forgotten to feed and walk her dogs.

There are many situations in life that require us to control our behavior, that is, use self-control. For example, if you're overweight and hate the way you look and feel, you need to learn how to control your eating.

Or if it's important for you to get in shape for a track meet, but you're smoking two packs of cigarettes a day, you need to learn how to stop smoking.

Here are some other situations that require self-control:

- When someone offers you alcohol or drugs
- When you have to decide about having sex with someone
- When you want to hit someone who has hurt you
- When you feel like skipping class or not showing up to work

Getting control over the strong emotions that these situations bring on is not easy.

Why is self-control so difficult? Why can't we decide just to "say no"? Why is it so hard to stop doing things

even when we want to stop? There are several answers to these questions.

It is difficult to control actions that give us immediate pleasure, like eating or smoking or drinking. Many of our friends do these things and we want them to accept us. Sometimes we do things that aren't good for us because we think it makes us look good.

Sometimes it is simply impossible to resist. Drugs, cigarettes, and alcohol can be physically addictive. If you use them enough, you get hooked. Your body needs them. If that happens, you need to seek help from a doctor or other professional.

Addictive habits are
always the hardest to give
up.

But for most people, self-control is something we can teach ourselves. It takes a lot of thinking, a lot of planning, and a lot of work. The payoff is getting a handle on your life and being able to achieve your goals. If Suzanne Watson can learn self-control, she'll become the veterinarian she wants to be.

Sooner or later, everybody has to learn to control his or her behavior. It doesn't matter how much money you have, where you live, or how you look. Betty Ford, the wife of former President Gerald Ford, battled drugs and alcohol for a good portion of her life. After the Fords left the White House, she went to a clinic in Rancho Mirage, California, that helped her control her life. The clinic, which is named after her now, helps thousands of people who are addicted to drugs and alcohol.

To learn how to control yourself, an important first step is to take a good, hard look at yourself. First Lady Betty Ford would tell you that, and she learned the hard way.

You can learn a lot about who you are by asking yourself questions about your behavior.

2

LEARNING ABOUT YOURSELF

BY TAKING A GOOD, HARD LOOK AT YOURSELF, you'll be on your way to gaining an important tool: self-knowledge.

What can self-knowledge do for you? It can show you your strengths and weaknesses, show you how you interact with others, and identify your goals in life.

Why is self-knowledge so important to self-control? Because it can show you what triggers problems that can lead you to lose control.

Before going to parties or school dances, Jonathan always took a couple of swigs of bourbon. He carried a flask in his hip pocket and frequently drank from it throughout the evening.

When Jonathan wasn't drinking and when he was honest with himself, he admitted that he didn't like the taste of alcohol. He didn't like the way it made him feel at the end of a long night or the next morning. He didn't even like the way it made him act while he was at parties. He thought drinking forced him to put on an act. He felt he often made a fool of himself.

Because Jonathan didn't like much about alcohol or what it did to him, he decided he wanted to stop drinking. He took a look at his drinking habits and tried to figure out what made him drink.

One of the first things Jonathan realized was that he often tried to avoid meeting or being with people. He didn't feel he knew what to say or that he fit in. So he used alcohol to make himself relax before he had to socialize. Alcohol made Jonathan feel "looser."

In small doses, alcohol seems to have a calming effect. But as he continued drinking, Jonathan found that he turned into a loud clown. He lost his self-control. Wild and uncontrolled was something the real Jonathan wasn't. It was a part he didn't want to play. The clown act was very different from his quiet personality.

Jonathan didn't like the way drinking changed his behavior. He also didn't like the way he felt after a night of heavy drinking. But after taking a hard look at himself, he realized that he drank because it helped him overcome his shyness.

When Jonathan asked himself why he was so nervous at parties, he realized that it was the people he was hanging around with that made him feel self-conscious and tense.

Many kids in his group drank and did drugs. And they seemed to like Jonathan because he drank and did drugs too. They liked the wild Jonathan clown.

By taking a hard look at himself, Jonathan identified the trigger that made him drink: peer pressure from the people he spent time with. He saw that pressure from the wrong kind of peers contributed to his need for alcohol. He was trying to impress the wrong people.

Jonathan realized he could stop abusing alcohol if he got rid of the trigger that made him drink. He saw that he needed to start spending time with people who didn't pressure him to drink or do drugs and who didn't expect him to put on a loud act. Jonathan set a goal for himself to get to know other people, people with whom he could be comfortable without alcohol or drugs.

Jonathan learned about himself—that he was shy. This shyness made him do things he didn't want to do when he was around people who made him uncomfortable. He then changed certain parts of his life—found new friends—and stopped drinking.

But how did Jonathan get self-knowledge? Did he just wake up one day, say "Eureka!" and there it was?

No. Jonathan went through a self-knowledge process:

• He asked himself questions. When do I drink? Why do I drink at only those times? Do I really like it?

• He asked others about how they saw him. He talked to a few old friends he trusted about the way they viewed his behavior.

• He learned from experience. Jonathan had experienced enough embarrassment and discomfort from his drinking to know that one more time was too many.

Asking questions about your behavior can help you gain self-knowledge. It can also help you use self-control when you need it most: when you must decide that you don't want to do something.

Here is a mental checklist that will help you avoid doing something you don't want to do:

• What will happen to me if I do this?
• What happened to me the last time I did this?
• Will I be able to stop doing this if I do it again?
• How will this affect the way others see me?
• Can I do this in a controlled way, or will I lose control?
• Will doing this make me feel good—only to feel terrible tomorrow?
• Will doing this ruin or delay a goal I really want to achieve?

Strong temptations can often make you forget your true goals.

Resisting your temptations is a rewarding experience that makes you feel good about yourself.

• Whom else am I hurting by doing this besides myself?

Add other questions to the list that you think you need to ask yourself.

The following are some problems that need self-control and some ways they might be handled.

Stay away from people and situations that tempt you. For example, if you're trying to stop smoking, stay away from individuals or groups you know will blow smoke in your face. During the early days, success may come more easily if you avoid the temptation.

Do the same if you are trying to lose weight. For example, Alicia, through self-knowledge, has determined that eating is her downfall. She simply cannot control herself when she sees or smells a bakery or ice cream shop, or when there are cookies and cakes in the kitchen.

Alicia controls her urges by changing her daily route to school, which passes by two bakeries she loves, a hot dog vendor, and an ice cream parlor. She also makes sure that she isn't alone in the kitchen. She leaves the table while the other people in her family are eating fattening foods. She cuts down on her television watching because it seems that every commercial shows tempting images of the fast foods and junk foods she likes. But she doesn't starve herself. She makes sure she has plenty of low-calorie, healthy snacks around when she is hungry.

This is all hard to do, but it is very important to Alicia that she control her eating. She would like to become a scholarship student at a local ballet school. She knows her weight is a serious obstacle.

Keeping up with school work can also be a self-control problem. Let's say you're having a hard time buckling down to study for a big test. It's hard to concentrate for any length of time, and it's hard to say "no" to friends who distract you from studying with offers of ball games and movies.

You know that you've got to make good grades to get into the college you want to attend. You're simply at a loss as to how to control yourself.

Here, too, you can help yourself by avoiding triggers that tempt you to do something you don't want to do. Find a place to study where it is quiet and no one will bother you. Commit yourself daily to that place at a set time. Avoid friends who don't appreciate your commitment. It will help to schedule time for leisure activities with people who do respect your need for regular study.

Sex is another part of your life where self-control may be a big issue. Feeling that you are in love and wanting to have sex with somebody can test your self-control. Sexual drives can be very strong—sometimes stronger

It helps to remember that self-control now will pay off in the future.

than you are. You have to think about what could happen after you have sex.

Here's a mental checklist to help you keep your self-
control when you want to have sex with someone you
care about:

• Do you have birth control? Are you prepared for
the consequences of an unplanned pregnancy?
• Will you or your partner use a condom? Condoms
can help prevent sexually transmitted diseases such as
AIDS or herpes.
• Are you emotionally prepared for sex? Sexual inti-
macy can set loose some powerful emotions. Can you
and your partner deal with them?

Remember, self-knowledge is the first step in self-
control. By taking a hard look at yourself, you can identify triggers that test your self-control. Maintain self-control by avoiding those triggers and using a mental checklist.

But what if you simply can't stop doing something
even though you really want to? Then you may have a
problem called addiction. That is a problem that makes
self-control almost impossible without professional help.

3

ADDICTION

WHAT IS ADDICTION?

Addiction is a word that means a lot of different things. If you like soft drinks a lot, you might tell people that you're "addicted to diet soda." But is that the same thing as being addicted to alcohol or drugs?

Obviously there is a difference. There are two kinds of addiction: mental and physical. Mental addiction is all in your head—for example, craving diet soda. Physical addiction is much more serious. Your body has to have whatever it is you're addicted to. If you're physically addicted to alcohol, for example, your body needs alcohol to function just as much as it needs food and water.

It can be hard to tell the difference between mental and physical addiction. Often mental addiction comes before physical addiction. If, for example, you use alcohol to relieve feelings of anxiety and depression, you probably are psychologically dependent on alcohol. You may not yet be physically addicted—although eventually you will be if you keep drinking heavily. It's the same with cigarettes and drugs. You can be doing a lot of drugs or smoking a lot of cigarettes and still not be physically addicted.

So how do you know if you're physically addicted to something?

First, only certain substances are known to be physically addictive. You can't become physically addicted to potato chips or hamburgers. But alcohol and most drugs can be physically addictive.

You are physically addicted if you can't stop drinking or doing drugs. If you have a constant craving for alcohol, for example, and you need more and more of it to satisfy your need—then you've become physically addicted. You will experience physical symptoms of withdrawal when you can't get alcohol. You may feel nauseated, your hands may shake, and you may have trouble sleeping.

The most common physically addictive substances are cigarettes, caffeine, alcohol, and drugs.

Many "everyday" drugs—like alcohol, nicotine, and caffeine—can easily become addictive with regular use.

Your self-control—or lack of it—can often be seen by looking at the things around you.

Cigarettes

One third of Americans are addicted to cigarettes, which contain the addictive substance nicotine. Nicotine is the active ingredient in tobacco. It raises blood pressure and negatively affects the heart and nervous system. Smoking is also linked to lung diseases such as emphysema and lung cancer.

Alcohol

When someone is addicted to alcohol, he or she is considered to be an alcoholic. Alcohol abuse is probably the most destructive addiction in the United States. There are over ten million alcoholics in the United States. One out of four homes is affected by an alcohol-related family problem. One in every three preteens or teens experiences some negative consequence of alcohol abuse every year, according to the National Council on Alcoholism. Half of the fifty thousand people who die annually in car accidents are killed by drunk drivers.

Drugs

Marijuana, cocaine, crack, and designer drugs such as "Ecstasy" and "China White" are all addictive. The stronger the drug, the more addictive it is. Physical addiction is possible after just a few hits of most drugs, particularly crack. And using, buying, or selling these drugs is illegal.

Addictions and a lack of
self-control together have
caused many lives to end
in ruin.

Prescription drugs are not illegal, but many of them can be addictive and must be handled with care. For example, codeine, a widely prescribed painkiller, can be habit-forming.

How do you know if you'll become addicted to something? You can't know for sure, but research offers some clues.

Doctors and scientists have spent a lot of time studying why people become addicts. They have discovered that addiction runs in families. If a person comes from a family where one or both parents are alcoholics, for example, that person has a greater risk of developing a drinking problem. In fact, studies show that the children of alcoholics have a four times greater risk of becoming alcoholics than the children of nonalcoholics.

Actress Drew Barrymore starred in the movie *E.T.* at the age of seven. By the age of nine she was addicted to alcohol, marijuana, and cocaine. She was the fifth generation of her movie star family to fall victim to these addictive substances.

Why is it easier to become an alcoholic or a drug addict if someone in your family is one?

Many scientists believe that we inherit our tolerance for addictive substances from our parents. That is especially true of alcohol.

If a person inherits a high tolerance for alcohol, he or she can drink a lot before feeling the effects. Alcoholics have been shown to have a high tolerance for alcohol. They don't have an early "cut-off point." A normal drinker has an early cut-off point. He or she is not able to drink a lot before feeling sick or very drunk. This type of person is unlikely to become an alcoholic.

Scientists believe the cut-off point is inherited in the same way that eye color or hair color are inherited. That's one way family history plays a role in alcoholism.

The emotional history of a family also affects the people within it. If a parent has a drinking problem, chances are that a lot of secrets and cover-ups exist in the family. People may not trust each other. That is what doctors call "dysfunctional" behavior.

If you come from this kind of background, you may have problems with your parents that are hard to work out. You may try to handle those problems by drinking. That's natural because that's what you learned at home.

All this doesn't mean you'll automatically become an alcoholic if one of your parents has a drinking problem. But it does mean you should think long and hard before using alcohol or other addictive substances.

At the same time, don't think you don't need to watch your drinking just because your parents have never had a problem with alcohol.

Some doctors also believe that your personality plays a role in whether you become addicted to alcohol or other substances. Psychiatrists have identified a certain type of personality called an "addictive personality."

Can you really have a type of personality that can cause you to become addicted more easily? And what is that type of personality?

If you're the type of person who is easily influenced by others, you may become addicted more easily. If you don't know your own mind and are lacking in self-knowledge, you may be at risk. Always looking for the easy way out and being unable to resolve your frustrations and problems constructively are two other signs of an addictive personality.

If any of this sounds like you, you need to be especially careful about using addictive substances. But remember that *only a doctor can determine whether you have an addictive personality*. Don't fall into the trap of deciding you have an addictive personality and using that as an excuse for your behavior.

You've been reading in this chapter about the problem of addiction—not being able to control your behavior even when you want to. It may surprise you to learn that some people have the opposite problem. They are too controlled. Interestingly, the effect is just as negative and self-destructive as addiction.

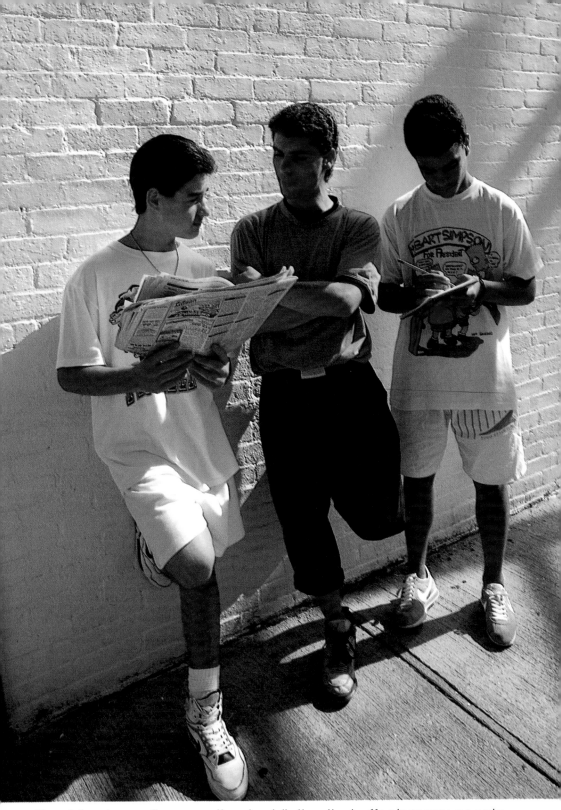

Gambling is an often unnoticed addiction that affects many people.

The singer Karen Carpenter died from heart damage caused by illnesses called anorexia nervosa and bulimia. The daughter of singer Pat Boone, Sherry Boone O'Neill, almost died from the same diseases.

Instead, Ms. O'Neill lived to tell the story of her life-threatening eating disorder in a book called *Starving for Attention*.

In her teens, Ms. O'Neill faced the possible financial ruin and divorce of her parents. At the same time, they disapproved of many of the things she did. They didn't like the way she dressed, the people she hung out with, or how she acted. In fact, it seemed to Ms. O'Neill that her parents didn't like anything about her.

Ms. O'Neill felt as if she was losing control—of her family, friends, and most important, her sense of personal identity.

So she rebelled. But she did it in an unusual way. Instead of losing control of herself in a sea of alcohol and drugs, she imposed too much control over herself. She stayed away from alcohol and drugs, but, unfortunately, she stayed away from healthy things as well.

Like Karen Carpenter, Ms. O'Neill denied herself food. She felt that by rigidly controlling her eating and weight she had power over her life and drew deserved attention to herself.

Ms. O'Neill went for days without eating anything. In addition, she tried to burn off calories through strenuous exercise. When she did eat, she often forced herself to vomit afterwards. Consequently, her weight fell from 120 pounds to below 80 pounds. When she was twenty-one, Ms. O'Neill almost died from the effects of her disorder.

People suffering from anorexia nervosa and bulimia try to control themselves totally. They often feel that their parents will love them only if they are perfect. If they are skinny, they think, their parents will love them more. Rejecting food is a way for these people to control the people around them.

It is interesting to note that anorexics and bulimics sometimes become addicted to alcohol or drugs. They try to cover up their guilt feelings about not eating by drinking or using narcotics. Having several serious problems like anorexia and alcohol abuse is called cross-addiction.

Anorexia and bulimia are examples of what happens if you exert too much control over your behavior. You need self-control, but you also have to remember that you are human. No one is perfect. Everyone has faults. If you overdo self-control and try to correct all your faults, you will never be happy with yourself. You will become depressed. You will stop communicating with others and getting out and enjoying life.

Singer-musician Karen Carpenter was anorexic. She exercised too much self-control and starved herself to death.

Support groups and counselors are important for people who need help setting healthy goals.

At worst, you may even think of ending your life. You will think that if you end your life, you can end your problems. If that sounds like you, you must seek help immediately.

There are some people who can learn self-control on their own—and there are a lot of people who can't. If you're an addict, alcoholic, anorexic or bulimic, severely depressed or suicidal, your problem is bigger than you are. It is important to recognize that you need help. *Get counseling right away.*

Here are some places to go for help:

- Your parents or other trusted members of your family
- A school counselor, psychologist, or social worker
- A clinic, halfway house, or rehabilitation center
- A doctor (such as a general practitioner or your family doctor)
- A doctor who is a specialist such as a psychiatrist or psychologist
- A certified support group such as Alcoholics Anonymous or for teens, Alateen (the National Council on Alcoholism has a toll-free number for information: 800-NCA-CALL.)

Taking the first step to get help is all-important toward helping yourself. But, there are places and people to avoid when seeking help:

• Friends who say, "Hey, do this! That's what I did, and it worked for me!" That doesn't mean it will work for you. Seek parental or professional help instead when you have a problem.

• Cults or "gurus" who promise to ease you out of your addiction with mystical methods. Groups like this can cost you a lot of money. And after a while they begin to control you. Self-control is no longer even a possibility.

• Newspaper or magazine advertisements that promise "miracle cures." Absolutely not. There is nothing miraculous about gaining or regaining self-control. It is hard work.

4

SUCCESS STARTS WITH SELF-CONTROL

A TELEVISION ADVERTISEMENT SHOWS BASKETBALL PLAYERS, mountain climbers, and bicycle riders excelling at their chosen sports. The slogan for the ad, which sells Nike brand footwear, is: "Little goals I've worked toward. They add up. Just do it."

Easy for them to say, you might think. And yet, what this ad is about, other than selling sneakers, is getting your act together. It's about getting and using self-control to achieve goals.

Having self-control means more than just recognizing and controlling bad habits. Self-control can also help you achieve your goals in life. It can get you something you really want. It can help you become the person you really want to be.

Let's say you want to excel in sports. You need self-control to be in good physical shape, work with a team, control anger or negative feelings that may take away from your concentration and performance, play by the rules, and avoid alcohol and drugs.

Most people who have reached the top of their chosen sport will tell you it took all those things to make it. And without self-control they couldn't have achieved them.

By 1982, Martina Navratilova, the international women's tennis star, had won every major professional tennis tournament in her eight-year career except one: the U.S. Open.

It was very important to Navratilova to win this major tournament. Yet she lost it year after year.

"Why?" she asked herself. After all, Martina had the discipline and self-control to leave her native land of Czechoslovakia for a new life in America and make it as a tennis star.

She analyzed herself mentally, emotionally, and physically all over again. She changed her diet. She got a new coach. She increased her hand-eye coordination drills and daily workouts. And she ended relationships that she felt were keeping her from achieving her goal.

In 1983, a year after she made these major changes in her life, she coolly and easily won the U.S. Open.

Setting up challenges for yourself, and then meeting them, is a great way to feel in control of your life.

Martina said of herself at that time, "I was, early in my career, impulsive and acted on feelings. I never took the time to think about what [was] really going on inside."

Jackie Robinson, the legendary Brooklyn Dodger, also got to the top by displaying self-control.

In 1947, Robinson was the first black man ever to play major league baseball. More times than he would care to remember he had to control his anger against teammates and crowds who taunted him with racial jeers and threats—even spat on him.

Joe Garagiola, the sports announcer, was once a teammate of Robinson's. In his book, *Jackie Robinson, A Life Remembered,* author Maury Allen interviewed Garagiola about Robinson. Garagiola said:

> **"Jackie took an awful lot of heat in those early years. I don't know of another player who could have handled that and not exploded. I mean they called him every name you could imagine and threw at him and cut him and did everything to run him out of the league. There should be a special place in baseball recognizing Jackie for more than just his baseball ability. He was a very special man."**

Through self-control and ability, Jackie Robinson persevered and rose to the top of his profession. His example paved the way for Willie Mays, Reggie Jackson, and all the other black superstars who followed him in baseball.

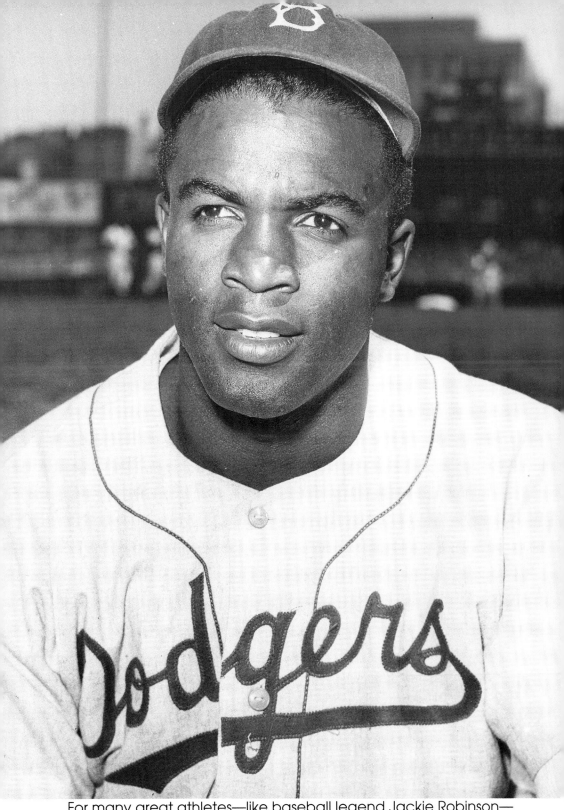

For many great athletes—like baseball legend Jackie Robinson—
success is a combination of self-control and ability.

Alcohol or drug abuse has threatened the careers of many sports stars. But for many others, self-control helped them overcome their problems.

In his second year as a pitcher for the New York Mets, Dwight Gooden had a record of 24 wins and only 4 losses. Many called him the best pitcher of all time.

But Gooden went into a slump and tested positive for cocaine use. He signed himself into a rehabilitation clinic for a month. Gooden recognized his problem, got treatment, and is now back playing quality baseball.

Other athletes also have learned the benefits of self-control. John Lucas, a guard with the Houston Rockets basketball team, had his own problem with drugs. So did two of his teammates, Lewis Lloyd and Mitchell Wiggins. But all three have been through successful rehabilitation. They now have another chance to live happy lives playing the sport they love.

Through the control these athletes learned by confronting their drug problems, they are playing better basketball and are in better shape than ever before. Houston is the only team in the National Basketball Association to carry three players who have been treated for drug problems during their careers.

Other athletes have not been as fortunate. Both Pete Rose and Denny McLain lost their careers to compulsive gambling. McLain, a superstar Detroit Tigers pitcher in the late 1960s, went on to heavy drinking, financial problems, and eventually prison.

Pete Rose, the celebrated Cincinnati Reds manager, was expelled from the game of baseball for the rest of his life. He may never gain the Baseball Hall of Fame status he is considered worthy of as an athlete.

Rose placed bets on baseball games, including Reds games. That's illegal for a professional baseball player. Although he knew what he was doing, he couldn't stop. Worse, he denied doing it. He became addicted to both gambling and lying.

In 1988 at the Summer Olympics in Seoul, South Korea, track star Ben Johnson was stripped of a gold medal after he tested positive for drug use. Johnson was using anabolic steroids. Steroids help an athlete perform despite an injury, and they increase muscle strength.

Johnson was a great athlete on his own, but his use of drugs made him run even faster. Unfortunately, it also made him fail his drug test. He lost both his medal and his reputation.

Some athletes have even lost their lives as a result of drug problems. Len Bias, the All-American basketball player from the University of Maryland, and Don Rogers, a defensive back for the Cleveland Browns football team,

both died suddenly. Bias, who was only twenty-three, suffered heart failure. Doctors determined that both deaths were related to cocaine abuse.

There are similar stories from the entertainment world. Consider the comedian John Belushi and musicians Jim Morrison, Jimi Hendrix, and Janis Joplin. They all lost their lives to drug and alcohol abuse. Singers Boy George and Belinda Carlisle are in rehabilitation and will probably be there for the rest of their lives.

Pete Rose's addiction to
gambling damaged his
career in baseball and
his personal life.

Former American Ballet Theatre ballerina Gelsey
Kirkland wrote a book called *Dancing on My Grave*
about her anorexia/bulimia and cocaine addiction. She
almost died—but saved herself by seeking help.

Why do so many athletes and celebrities succumb to
the lure of drugs and alcohol?

Being in the spotlight—either in sports or show busi-
ness—puts you in a very fast and glamorous world. You
are subject to pressure from both peers and fans to live in
the fast lane at all times. Partying is a big part of life. At
the same time, a lot of athletes and celebrities are vulner-
able to peer pressure because they are young and don't
know themselves.

Moreover, athletes often believe they are immune to
the dangers of alcohol and drugs because they are so
strong physically. Some athletes also mistakenly think
alcohol and drugs make them perform better by either
relaxing or energizing them. They feel they must win at
all costs. But as we have seen, careers and lives can be
ruined through the use of drugs and alcohol.

What if you aren't planning to become a famous athlete or rock star? Can self-control still help you achieve
your goals? Absolutely. Whatever your goals in life, you
will always be presented with problems, choices, and
challenges. If you have a firm grip on who you are and

what you want, you will be less likely to make the wrong choices and bring on the worst problems.

Yes, you need self-control to gain and keep fame and fortune. But you need self-control just as much to be successful in school, to get along in friendships and family relationships, and to perform well in any job you take on. Judy's story is a good example.

Judy likes her job as a nurse's aide. She knows she is good at it because she is the teaching supervisor in her department. She's famous for knowing her stuff.

But in a recent evaluation Judy was criticized by both supervisors and patients. They said she "gets angry too fast," "flies off the handle," and "takes everything too personally." A promotion to enter the registered nurse training program was not recommended.

"I do not!" thought Judy angrily as she read through her evaluation. Yet her boyfriend Peter often made the same complaint. "You get mad at me too fast, without giving me a chance to explain," he had told her many times when they argued. She knew her relationship with Peter was in trouble. She really loved Peter, but she just wasn't getting along with him. It seemed to be getting worse and worse.

"I've had it with these people—every single one of them," Judy told a favorite aunt. "The supervisors want one thing. The patients buzz me all day long for nothing.

Holding down a regular job, and doing it well, requires discipline and self-control.

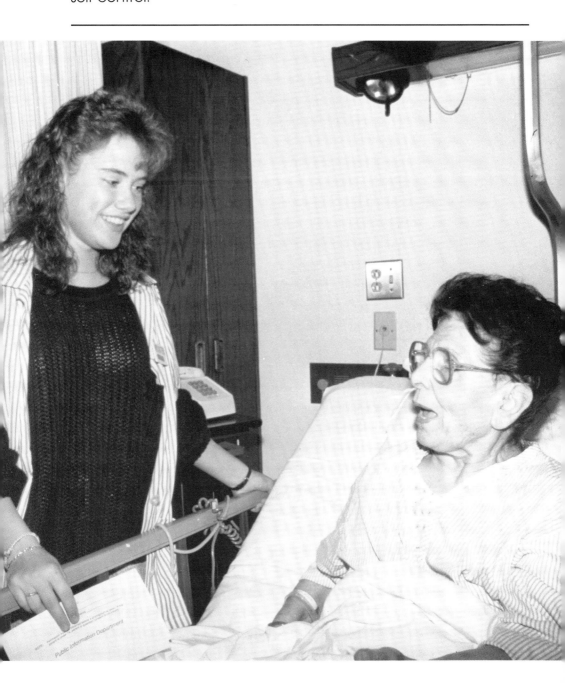

Peer groups can often make you feel pressure to do things you would normally avoid.

Peter's never happy with me. He says I flare up too easily. The heck with all of them."

Judy's aunt gently suggested that Judy had something to think about. She was having a lot of problems that all seemed connected with her losing her temper. Judy's future—professional and personal—was at stake here. Her aunt gave her the name of a good therapist she knew and suggested that she call.

Judy began to see the therapist regularly. Through these sessions, she began to learn a lot about her anger and herself. She learned that she had low self-esteem. That meant that she didn't believe in herself. She lacked confidence. When someone criticized her, she immediately took it personally instead of coolly evaluating the criticism. Her anger covered up her insecurity.

Judy also learned that she became angry too quickly. When a patient bothered her with unnecessary requests, or a supervisor acted in a way Judy thought was unfair, she immediately became resentful. She had to learn to behave more calmly in such situations.

Talking to her therapist, Judy learned how to change her behavior:

• She worked on improving her self-esteem. She stopped feeling like a victim all the time.

- She began to use relaxation techniques to keep herself from getting angry. These included meditating, listening to music, giving herself instructions to calm down, counting to ten, or just telling herself she was O.K.

- She stopped taking criticism personally and stopped holding grudges.

- She worked on keeping her sense of humor whenever possible.

- She discovered that there is a time for anger and a time to control anger.

In other words, Judy learned self-control. Her efforts paid off. Judy's coworkers began to appreciate her more. So did her boyfriend. Her job and her personal life improved.

Judy was lucky in that she didn't have a problem with drinking or drugs. She only lacked emotional self-control. But sometimes that can be as serious as a drinking or drug problem.

Recently, eighty-seven lives were lost in a tragic fire in New York City because one man lacked emotional self-control. Julio Gonzalez set fire to the nightclub where his girlfriend worked because she had rejected him. Nearly everyone in the club died.

Fortunately, such tragedies are rare. But they remind us of the importance of self-control in our lives. Whatever your goals, self-control is the key to success. Whether you're trying to get a job you want, train for an athletic event, or just get along with a boyfriend or boss, you have to learn to control your behavior to reach your goals.

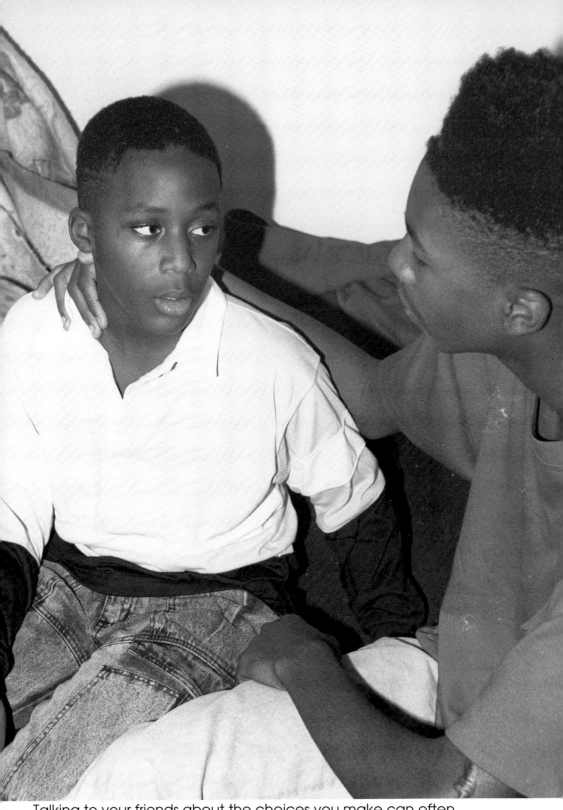

Talking to your friends about the choices you make can often help you to better understand your behavior.

5

CAN YOU TEACH WHAT YOU'VE LEARNED?

IF YOU HAVE LEARNED SELF-CONTROL AND CREATED POSITIVE change in your life, you might try to help a friend face a problem.

But do it constructively. Make sure, first of all, that the friend is seriously interested in changing his or her situation.

Tell your friend how you handled a similar situation that required self-control. And introduce him or her to groups or specialists who had helped you.

You might also form an informal support group with a few friends to discuss self-control and common goals.

If you plan an informal group, it's important to follow some guidelines:

- Listen as well as talk.
- Be honest if you've had some trouble with self-control recently.
- Arrange a group activity that would be helpful to members' goals.
- Don't be too hard on group members who are having problems.

Remember, nobody is perfect, and finding your way to self-control can be a long and difficult journey.

When trying to help a friend or someone in your family, don't take on problems such as addiction that are too big to handle. Encourage professional counseling. You can provide names, phone numbers, and encouragement.

If you can consider helping a friend with a self-control problem, you're probably in pretty good shape yourself. You've learned how to get in touch with yourself, your needs, and your goals.

Having mastered a particular self-control problem, however, you can never get too comfortable. No one can. Anyone who has achieved goals in life knows there are many setbacks and challenges along the way. He or she also has the mental tools to work out the problems that may arise.

Self-control is a lifelong process. But it will become easier as you get older. You'll be able to draw on your experience in solving old problems to meet new challenges. You'll have confidence in yourself and your abilities. Most important, you'll have the satisfaction of knowing that your self-control gives you power over your own life.

Glossary: *Explaining New Words*

addiction Compulsive use of and growing tolerance for a substance. Addiction can be mental or physical depending on the substance and the person's needs.

addictive drugs Marijuana, cocaine, crack, heroin, Ecstasy, and China White are just some of the drugs considered addictive. Prescriptive drugs such as codeine, a painkiller, are also considered addictive.

addictive personality A type of personality likely to become addicted.

alcoholism Inability to control your intake of alcoholic beverages, including beer, wine, and hard liquors such as vodka, gin, bourbon, and scotch.

anorexia nervosa   An emotional disorder characterized by an aversion to food. The anorexic regularly avoids food, regardless of hunger. Unless treated, the disorder can result in death from starvation.

bulimia   Frequent overeating that results in physical and emotional discomfort and is relieved by throwing up.

cross-addiction   Answering one addictive problem with another. For example, things to make yourself feel better about your anorexia problem by drinking too much or taking drugs.

cut-off point   The point at which your system reacts to alcohol by becoming intoxicated, or sick. If you have an early cut-off point, you can drink only a limited amount before feeling the effects of alcohol. If you have a late cut-off point, you can drink a lot before feeling the effects. Alcoholics tend to have a late cut-off point.

dysfunctional behavior   A type of behavior that develops in reaction to your own addiction or self-control problems, or those in your family. Examples of dysfunctional behavior include secretiveness, lying, and denial of bad habits.

nicotine   The habit-forming chemical in cigarettes that raises blood pressure and negatively affects the heart and nervous system.

self-control   The ability to control our behavior. There are many situations in life that require us to use self-control.

self-knowledge   The ability to know your strengths and weaknesses. Self-knowledge is an important tool in learning how to control yourself.

suicide   The taking of one's own life. It usually happens when someone is feeling sad, inadequate, or hopeless. The person feels that his or her life is out of control.

tolerance   The need for increasing amounts of a substance to produce the same effect on the body with regular use. "High tolerance" means your system can handle increasing amounts with very little effect. "Low tolerance" means that you will feel effects very fast and not be able to absorb increases easily.

trigger   A situation or activity that makes it hard for you to control yourself. Passing by a bakery that smells good when you're trying to stay on a diet is a "trigger."

For Further Reading

Allen, Maury. *Jackie Robinson, A Life Remembered.* New York, Toronto: Franklin Watts, 1987.

Anderson, Louie. *Dear Dad—Letters from an Adult Child.* New York: Viking, 1989.

Berry, James. *Heroin Was My Best Friend.* New York: Crowell-Collier Press, 1971.

Dolan, Edward F. *Drugs in Sports.* New York: Franklin Watts, 1986.

Hyde, Margaret O. *Addictions: Gambling, Smoking, Cocaine Use and Others.* New York: McGraw-Hill Book Co., 1978.

Hyde, Margaret O., and Forsyth, Elizabeth H., M.D. *AIDS—What Does It Mean to You?* New York: Walker, 1987.

Ketcham, Katherine, and Gustafson, Ginny Lyford. *Living on the Edge: A Guide to Intervention for Families with Drug and Alcohol Problems.* New York: Bantam, 1989.

Kirkland, Gelsey with Greg Lawrence. *Dancing on My Grave.* New York: Doubleday, 1986.

Miller, Caroline Adams. *My Name Is Caroline.* New York: Doubleday, 1988.

Navratilova, Martina with George Vecsey. *Martina.* New York: Knopf, 1985.

O'Neill, Sherry Boone. *Starving for Attention.* New York: Continuum, 1982.

Otis, Carol L., M.D. and Goldinggay, Roger. *Campus Health Guide: The College Student's Handbook for Healthy Living.* New York: College Entrance Examination Board, 1989.

Wells-Brandon, Carla. *Eat Like a Lady: A Guide for Overcoming Bulimia.* Deerfield Beach, FL: Health Communications Inc., 1989.

INDEX

Index

About the Author

Maggie Kneip has worked as a public relations executive and as a dance teacher and choreographer. She currently lives in New Jersey, where she is a freelance writer and mother of two children.

Photo Credits and Acknowledgments

Cover Photo: Barbara Kirk
Photos on pages 2,6,10,12, 18,32,41: Mary Lauzon; page 17: Barbara Kirk; pages 21,49: Stephanie FitzGerald; pages 25,26–27,36, 50, 54: Stuart Rabinowitz; page 28: Bruce Glassman; pages 35 and 43: Wide World Photo.

Design and Production: Blackbirch Graphics, Inc.